For Kaztah

First published 2007 by Walker Books Ltd
87 Vauxhall Walk, London SE11 5HJ

This edition published 2008

10 9 8 7 6 5 4 3 2 1

© 2007 Sue Heap

The right of Sue Heap to be identified as author/illustrator
of this work has been asserted by her in accordance with the
Copyright, Designs and Patents Act 1988

This book has been typeset in Franklin Gothic.
Handlettering by Sue Heap.

Printed in China

British Library Cataloguing in Publication Data: a catalogue
record for this book is available from the British Library

ISBN 978-1-4063-1334-5 (with drawing book)
ISBN 978-1-4063-1615-5

www.walkerbooks.co.uk

WALKER BOOKS
AND SUBSIDIARIES
LONDON · BOSTON · SYDNEY · AUCKLAND

Danny's
Drawing
Book

by Sue Heap

ZO

TICKETS

I'm Danny. This is me
with my yellow drawing book.
Next to me is my friend Ettie.
And this is how we made a story
when we went to the zoo
on a snowy day.

ENTRANCE

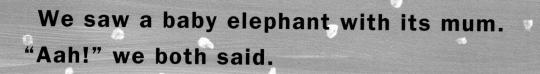

We saw a baby elephant with its mum.
"Aah!" we both said.

Near the elephants, a red scarf
was hanging in a tree.
I drew the baby elephant all cosy
and warm in the red scarf.
But Ettie and I were blue with cold...

...so we went into the Nocturnal Animal House. That's where the night-time animals live. Slowly, our eyes got used to the dark and there in front of us was one of the most special animals we'd ever seen.

Ettie read the sign. "He's an aardvark and he comes from Africa. He lives underground in a burrow." "Hello, aardvark!" we whispered.

I drew the
aardvark next
to the elephant.

"I think they
really like
each other,"
said Ettie.

And she was right!

I decided the aardvark would like a green hat, so I drew him one. Then I added a suitcase and some buns for the elephant.

The aardvark said he was going to Africa.
The elephant wanted to go too.

But they didn't know how to get there.

The elephant had some ideas.

But the aardvark didn't like them.

I told them I could help, but Ettie and I wanted to come too. So I drew us in my drawing book.

And
then I
drew ...

a beautiful plane to take us all the way there.

When we landed, we saw two giraffes,
a hippo and her baby, two lions, a rhino,
a monkey, a tiger and a snake.

The elephant found a herd of friends
to play with.

Ettie and I gave them buns.

But the poor aardvark
was too hot, so I drew ...

...a cool dark burrow deep underground.

Ettie and I danced and sang with the elephant while the aardvark played the trumpet.

Then it was time to go home. But the elephant and the aardvark wanted to stay in Africa.

So we hugged and kissed and said goodbye.

Ettie wondered how we'd get home,
but I knew exactly what to do ...

"That's what I call a happy ending!"
said Ettie as we left the zoo.
"Yes," I said. "I wonder what
we'll draw tomorrow."

The Burrow

Dear Danny and Ettie,
from deep down in my burrow
I send you spadefuls of love.
Aardvark

To Danny and Ettie
near the ZOO

c/o Walker Street
England

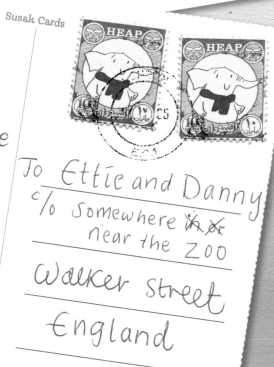

Dear Ettie and Danny,
I'm having a smashing time
with my new friends.
They all want a red scarf.
Love, Elephant
P.S. Could you send us some buns!

To Ettie and Danny
c/o Somewhere near
near the ZOO

Walker Street

England

WB 006

ZOO TICKET

CP 007

ZOO TICKET

Other books by
Sue Heap

ISBN 978-1-84428-554-9

ISBN 978-1-4063-1485-4

Available from all good bookstores

www.walkerbooks.co.uk